Mail Order
The Foundling's New Mother

By
Faith Johnson

Clean and Wholesome Western Historical Romance

Printed in the United States of America

Table of Contents

Unsolicited Testimonials

By **Glaidene Ramsey**
☆☆☆☆☆ I so enjoy reading Faith Johnson's stories. This Bride and groom met as she arrived in town. They were married and then the story begins.!!!! Enjoy

By **Voracious Reader**
☆☆☆☆☆ "Great story of love and of faith. The hardships we may have to go through and how with faith, and God's help we can get through them" -

By **Glaidene's reads**
☆☆☆☆☆ "Faith Johnson is a five star writer. I have read a majority of her books. I enjoyed the story and hope you will too!!!!!"

By **Kirk Statler**
☆☆☆☆☆ I liked the book. A different twist because she wasn't in contract with anyone when she went. She went. God provided for her needs. God blessed her above and beyond.

By **Amazon Customer**
☆☆☆☆☆ Great clean and easy reading, a lot of fun for you to know ignores words this is crazy so I'll not reviewing again. Let me tell it and go

By **Kindle Customer**
☆☆☆☆☆ Wonderful story. You have such a way of showing people that opposite do attack. Both in words and action. I am glad that I found your books.

FREE GIFT

Just to say thanks for checking our works we like to gift you

Our Exclusive Never Before Released Books

100% FREE!

Please GO TO

http://cleanromancepublishing.com/gift

And get your FREE gift

Thanks for being such a wonderful client.

Chapter One

Gwen Arnold was eating her last dinner at the family table before she left for Texas to be a mail-order bride. It had never been easy growing up as the oldest of ten children. In fact, there were many times Gwen forgot she was an older sister—instead, she felt like a mother.

After Gwen left, her eighteen-year-old sister, Lizzie, would take over most of her duties. Her responsibilities would become daunting when her big sister left, and Lizzie didn't talk to Gwen for days when she found out she was leaving Dartmouth, Massachusetts.

Gwen predicted she would follow a similar path to escape in a few years. She might not become a mail-order bride, but she'd figure something out.

Joshua Arnold, Gwen’s father, was a good man who worked hard as a dairy farmer. He owned the family farm with his brother Abe, who also had ten kids. Every day was a flurry of activity, and the Arnold brothers were not always sure which ten kids belonged to them. It was none of their faults, because it wasn’t easy when there were twenty children. Joshua and Abe likely saw twenty mouths to feed, which they managed.

After breakfast, most of the younger children went out to learn or do chores in the barn. Gwen was alone with her father as Lizzie cleared the dinner table. It was apparent that he wanted a word with his daughter before she departed the following day.

"Are you sure someone's going to be waiting for you in…" He paused. Gwen knew he had forgotten where she was going and helped him out.

"Yes, Andrew Carver is picking me up, and I trust his word. It's Fern Township, Texas, but it's easier if you just call it Fern," Gwen said as she pushed a chunk of her straight honey-colored hair out of her face. With her stringy hair and slight figure, Gwen looked younger than her years. However, she didn't mind it because she was secretly strong and liked that it surprised people.

"Like the name of your sister; that makes it easier." He smiled. He was referring to three-year-old Fern Arnold. "I know things haven't always been easy for you here in Dartmouth, and I hope you're leaving knowing that your mother and I did our very best. We should have given you more time to meet a fella so you wouldn't be resorting to becoming a mail-order bride."

"I know you did, Father, and I don't think I'm choosing Andrew out of desperation. Rather it's my way of seeking adventure. I leave Dartmouth with nothing but fond memories. I'm sure Lizzie and then Sue will take over my chores without a problem."

June Arnold, Gwen's mother, walked in and joined her husband at the table with eleven-month-old Isiah on her lap. "We're proud of the woman you've become and wish we could have offered more. Don't forget about us and write of your life in Texas."

"I will. I'll miss everyone in Dartmouth and carry all that you taught me," Gwen said.

"One thing is sure, you'll know how to care for babies when you have them," Mrs. Arnold said. "The Lord kept blessing me with babies, and it wouldn't have been easy without your help."

"I love every one of them, but I have a chance to live child-free for a time. So I'd like to at least get to know my husband and my new life in Texas before having babies," Gwen explained.

"Is Andrew of the same mind?" Gwen's mother inquired.

"I mentioned it, and he didn't say he was opposed, although having a family in the future is something he looks forward to. I'm only twenty-one years old, and you're proof that someone can keep having babies well into their thirties," Gwen said. "Once I start as a mother, there will be no chance for a break—not ever."

***

Gwen had never been to Boston before, and it was a smelly place compared to Dartmouth. Her father made sure she arrived at the train station on time and waited with her until it was time to board. Gwen had never felt so frightened and excited in her life. She squeezed her father as they shared a hug and tried to sear the moment into her memory. The chances were that she would never see June and Joshua Arnold again.

Gwen walked down the narrow path with benches on either side. A metal bar stuck up from the bench to separate it into individual spaces or seats. It was going to be a long cramped journey, and she hoped that the passenger next to her was interesting and clean. She couldn't imagine spending days next to a person who reeked and talked about boring subjects.

Then, Gwen reconsidered that because she didn’t think many subjects were boring. She loved to hear about things she knew nothing about, which was pretty much everything.

She took a seat next to a small window that was covered with a layer of soot inside and out.

Finally, a passenger took the seat next to her. Gwen knew of her condition because she had seen her mother pregnant on many occasions. Based on the size of her belly and the look of exhaustion on her face, it was clear that her baby would come along in a week or less. Gwen hoped the woman had a female traveling companion who was ready to help with the birth at a moment's notice.

"Hello, I'm Gwen Arnold. I'm going clear to Texas. Will you be my traveling companion for long?" she asked.

"I'll be getting off in Oklahoma. I'm Carrie McNeil," the young woman said as she struggled to get situated.

Gwen found the seat uncomfortable herself, and she couldn't imagine how Carrie felt.

"Are you going to be with family, a husband perhaps?" Gwen asked. Thinking it made sense, considering her condition.

"No. I don't have either. I was born in Oklahoma and thought it would be a good place to have my baby. There's an orphanage there where I was born, and I know the town well. I was working as a live-in maid in Boston, but my big belly started getting in the way of doing my job."

"Where will you stay if you don't know anyone?"

"The family I worked for in Boston was very generous when I left. I have enough money to stay in a guest house for a week, and then I hope to find work as a live-in nanny where I can bring my baby along," Carrie explained.

Gwen couldn't believe she had come upon someone more naïve than she was. Oklahoma wasn't Boston, and there wouldn't be many nanny or maid positions available. From what she knew, Oklahoma wasn't a very hospitable place, which would be made worse by Carrie's situation. Her uncle Ray had spent time out west, and he was most afraid of Oklahoma for a variety of reasons.

"I'd suggest you head to the first church you can find. You'll need protection from someone, and the church will give you direction."

"That's a good idea. Thank you for your advice," Carrie said.

Her deep-blue eyes and kind smile were endearing. Gwen wished she could do more for Carrie other than just dole out advice.

Chapter Two

Andrew Carver was up while most of the other cowboys were still snoring. As the foreman on the large Seager Ranch, he was supposed to have his own place to live or even a private room. Unfortunately, the foreman's cabin had burned down, and there was no extra room in the bunkhouse. Andrew didn't mind too much because the boys on the ranch were like a big family. Living with them only furthered their bond, and it hadn't been a problem until he had a wife on the way.

His buddy Colt had suggested he get a mail-order bride, and it didn't take too much convincing. Andrew was twenty-nine years old and hardly had time to scratch an itch, let alone meet a gal he'd like to marry. Colt pointed out that a man wasn't really a man until he had a nipper or two that would carry his name. So he started corresponding with Gwen from Massachusetts, who seemed just as eager to get on with married life. She had spent time around animals and children, making her a perfect fit for the life he imagined.

Andrew thought about what he had planned for the day as he poured himself a cup of strong coffee. First, he had to move the youngest cattle that hadn't been branded yet toward the barn. Poor things wouldn't know what hit them, but it was part of their life they'd soon forget.

"Morning, Andy," Colt said. He was the only person alive who got away with calling him the shortened version of his name. Andrew's beloved grandfather had called him Andy. "Tomorrow is the big day you pick Gwen up in Houston."

"Sure is, and I'll be gone for the day, so I'm relying on you to keep things straight around here. I didn't bother telling Mr. Seager, and I don't think he cares much as long as the cattle keep healthy and moving.

Colt pulled his hat down on his head as they walked from the bunkhouse to the barn together. The weather was dry in late spring after the torrential rains of February and March.

"The boys are clearing a corner of the bunkhouse for you and Gwen. Abner is looking for a sheet to hang to give you and the wife some privacy," Colt said.

"I appreciate how you and the boys are so welcoming of Gwen before you even meet her," Andrew remarked.

"It's all because you treat every one of us with respect. There isn't a foreman in Texas who men want to work for more than you. Many of them were down on their luck when they came here, and you helped make their lives better," Colt said.

"I ain't no better than any one of the cowboys in the bunk. My grandfather showed me the door when I was no more than seventeen and told me to make a man of myself. It was the right way to do it because I had no choice unless I wanted to die of hunger. I couldn't survive on squirrel over the fire. Patch Jenkins was the foreman who let me hop on one of his horses. I was lucky, and I like spreading my luck around," Andrew explained. "Being a cowboy is a better life than being an outlaw, which I could have easily become."

"Was Gwen serious about not wanting kids right away?" Colt asked.

Andrew nodded. "Not in the first year, at least. She wants a rest, and I figure I can wait; that way, we'll have our house built when we have a baby. Are you boys serious about helping build a one-bedroom place?"

"We sure are," Colt said enthusiastically. "Is it going to be where the old foreman's cabin stood?"

"Yup. Mrs. Seager wants it there because she says it's out of sight. She doesn't like to have to look at the help," Andrew pointed out. "Mr. Seager is mild-mannered, but she's the opposite, so I reckon they balance each other out."

He kicked the dirt just as Lottie Seager walked by. She used to be around the ranch every day before she got married and moved to the other side of the property. She had her father's easygoing personality, or at least she used to. However, Andrew noticed that lately, she scowled more than not and acted like she had a bee in her bonnet.

"Did you just kick dirt in my direction?" Lottie said. It was clear she was offended.

"Never, Miss Lottie," Andrew said. He used the way she asked to be addressed.

"You can call me Mrs. Scoggins." She walked away in a huff.

"I'd be careful of that one," Colt said to Andrew. "You don't want to get on the wrong side of the boss, and you know how protective fathers are about their girls.

"You ought to know. How's Sally, and is she fitting in good with your sister's family?" Andrew asked.

Colt nodded and tried smiling, but it was just a flat line. "She still misses her mom, although she loves her aunt Grace. When she was five, we could say stuff like she went for a long ride on the back of an angel. Now she gets it and knows her mom is dead. That's not something youngins should have to deal with."

"I was sixteen when my mother passed, and I could barely take it then. I give your little girl a lot of credit for dealing with so much turmoil. At least you get to see Sally, and she knows you're her father. Grace and Charlie know what they're doing with the five other children. I'd like Grace to meet Gwen, since she won't have any friends here in Fern," Andrew said.

Colt's wife had died suddenly. Something like a heart attack hit her with no hint that anything was wrong. She fell over, closed her eyes, and never woke up. Colt was heartbroken and didn't know how to raise Sally. His sister-in-law offered to take her in as her own and adopt her. That didn't work for Colt, who still wanted Sally to know he was her father. They worked out a situation, and everyone was as happy as they could be without Mary.

“I’ll saddle my horse and grab a couple of the boys to join us. Do you want the flank, back, or lead?" Colt asked.

“I’ll take the back where I can catch the little rascals that refuse to follow the herd,” Andrew said with a grin.

Chapter Three

The baby was pink and crying as she lay in Carrie's arms. Mrs. Galloway, who was sitting nearby, had helped with the birth, and they couldn't have done it without her. She had sixteen grandchildren and had helped bring most of them into the world. Gwen had seen her mother give birth in Dartmouth, but she had never taken such an active role. It was both beautiful and frightening.

After more than a week of travel, the train was about to cross the border into Oklahoma. Gwen hadn't had the time to worry about her husband-to-be, Andrew. In a way, that was a blessing because, without anything to do, Gwen would have spent time fretting. She wasn't sure exactly where in

Oklahoma Carrie and her baby girl were planning to depart. Gwen knew the duo would be cared for as long as she remembered to find the nearest church. She chuckled inside. It seemed babies were following her all the way to Fern; perhaps a message was being sent to her.

Mrs. Galloway sat on one side of Carrie and Gwen on the other. The new mother's eyes were closed, and the newborn was content with her eyes closed as well. It was a peaceful moment after the chaos that came along with having a baby on the train.

"Does this make you more or less excited for the arrival of your first?" Mrs. Galloway asked.

Gwen shrugged her shoulders. "I have seen many siblings and cousins being born, so this is nothing new. I do look forward to having a baby, but just not right away. But, if it does happen soon after I marry Andrew, then I suppose it's meant to be," Gwen responded.

Mrs. Galloway spoke in a quiet voice so as not to wake or concern Carrie. "I'm a little concerned that her color hasn't come back. She's white as a sheet compared to the baby's pink skin," she commented. "I hate that she doesn't have someone to meet her at the train depot. No one should have to be alone in this world."

Gwen nodded in agreement and proceeded to nudge a clearly worn-out Carrie. "You did a wonderful job, showing bravery and strength. Aside from being tired, are you feeling all right?"

Carrie blinked open her blue eyes. She slowly shook her head. "Call her Sara. Thank you both." She pointed her face down and kissed Sara. A faint smile came over her face before she went limp and little Sara began to cry.

Mrs. Galloway gently patted Carrie's face as Gwen took the infant in her arms. They repeated her name, and several other passengers rushed in to help. Carrie McNeil died with a smile on her face after bringing her baby into the world.

Gwen looked down at Sara, who cooed. Mrs. Galloway looked at Gwen, and they both nodded.

Sara was headed to Fern, Texas.

***

Andrew rode a wagon into Houston to pick up Gwen. He knew she was slender and would be wearing a yellow bonnet with tiny red flowers. Most passengers left after the long journey would have gotten off in Dallas, so he didn't think she would be difficult to find. Andrew sure wished he had a proper home for them, but that wouldn't be for some time. By the time they started having children, they would have a home.

Andrew stood at the train platform and watched as the passengers departed. He saw many men depart who were greeted by their families. His heart soared as he thought that he was soon to have a wife and eventual family of his own. One scene touched him because it was so beautiful. A woman walked off the train with a tiny baby in her arms. She was joined by an older woman who must have been her mother. Andrew smiled and breathed deeply before noticing something about the woman—she wore a yellow hat. Then, the older woman walked in the opposite direction.

Andrew tentatively approached the woman.

"Andrew, is that you?" she asked. "You're tall with a mustache and green eyes, which matches the description I have."

"I'm Andrew, and you must be Gwen. I'm very confused because you never mentioned a child. In fact, you said you needed a rest from little ones." He searched for words. "I guess you must be carrying the baby for another departing guest."

"No, You'll see a pine box being taken off the train, and that is sadly Sara's mother. It sounds indelicate, but it's true. The woman I was on the train with, Mrs. Galloway, will make sure Carrie has a dignified burial, and I said, um…that I would see to Sara. We'll find a good orphanage or home for her." Gwen let the words float between them.

"You've been traveling, and decisions can't be made when you're overwhelmed with exhaustion. We have a journey that will be at least a few hours. The baby, or Sara as you call her, will have to come along to Fern."

"This is not how I expected our first meeting to happen, and I'm very sorry," Gwen said.

"I don't know what you're sorry about. Unfortunately, a tragedy struck, and you stepped in to do something for this innocent child. If you had done otherwise, I would have had second thoughts about selecting you as my mail order bride."

"I suppose you're right. I didn't hesitate, and before she died, I even thought about bringing Carrie and Sara to Fern. I had no idea how you would have reacted, but I got to know Carrie; she had a good heart. She was raised in an orphanage and had no husband, but still, she had a positive way of looking at things," Gwen said.

"How were you feeding the baby on the train?" Andrew asked.

"A couple of women who still had milk after giving birth stepped in. However, she'll likely wake up wanting more in an hour," Gwen pointed out.

"We're taking a little detour so we can feed little Sara. Grace Cox had a nipper not too long ago, and if she can help, I know she'll do so," Andrew said.

"That would be wonderful. It will give us time to come up with something to feed her with using cow's milk."

"I can't remember when I've smiled so much. It has to be little Sara. I can't think of anything else," Andrew said. His eyes sparkled when he looked at the baby.

Gwen was smiling, too. Sara was having a similar effect on her, but she wondered if Andrew had even noticed her. It didn't feel much different than home in Dartmouth; when she was there, she just blended in. Gwen scolded herself for having such selfish feelings.

Chapter Four

Gwen followed Andrew into the small but cheery home. It gave her a warm feeling, and she could almost see love hanging in the air. It was a touch chaotic, but no one seemed to mind.

"Andrew," a woman said. She was surprised to have guests but didn't seem to mind one bit. She held a baby in her arms that couldn't have been more than one year old. "This must be Gwen. Colt didn't tell me you were stopping by, but I'm always glad to see you. Now, be a gentleman and introduce me to your bride-to-be and the precious package she's carrying."

Gwen spoke up and did the introduction. "I'm Gwen Arnold from

Dartmouth, Massachusetts, and this is Sara. She was just born yesterday. I'd explain, but the story is lengthy, and this situation got real confusing, real fast."

"No explanation necessary. I'm Grace Duffy, and my husband, Charlie, is the other adult wandering around the house. Five of these children are mine, and Sally officially belongs to Colt. That's also a confusing story that I'll let Andrew tell," Grace said. "Sara's fussy, and I figure this little one wants to eat."

"That's why we're here," Andrew butted in. "I was hoping that since you're feeding little Charles, you might not mind doing the same for Sara."

She reached for the baby without saying a word. "It is confusing, but I've never been one for details. Sara wants milk, and I have plenty."

A young girl who was no older than ten years jumped forward. "I'm Sally. My dad is Colt, but I live here because my mother died. Grace is like a new mother, although she's really my aunt."

Gwen explained the situation about Carrie dying on the train with no family. Grace fed the baby until she was satisfied and fell asleep. While the women were talking, Sally was sitting in Andrew's lap, asking questions about Colt, who Gwen wondered about. Grace figured she hadn't met Colt, so she filled Gwen in on her sister's death and how Sally came to live with the Duffy family. Grace taught her how to make a bottle out of a jelly jar that would work well enough for

Sara. She also promised to come by when she could and give her a good feed.

Gwen left feeling like she had made a friend in Texas. It gave her a warm feeling because her sister Lizzie was her only friend at Dartmouth. Everything was moving so fast for Gwen, but one thing was growing by the minute. That was the deep affection she had for Sara, which had appeared as soon as Carrie passed.

Andrew held Sara as Gwen climbed up on the wagon after their visit. He placed the baby in her arms, and for the first time, she got a close-up look at his face. His green eyes were unlike any he had seen. They were light and smiling. For a cowboy, his movements bordered on being graceful, not rough as she imagined they would be. Gwen shook her head, realizing her focus needed to be on Sara.

"We'll be at the Seager ranch in less than an hour," Andrew said. "I'll have just enough time to tell you something you weren't aware of."

"Oh, I hope you don't secretly have a wife whom you didn't tell me about," Gwen said jokingly, but inside she wasn't joking at all.

"Nothing like that, I assure you. I had a separate home on the ranch, but it burned to the ground, and since then, I've been living in the bunkroom with the cowboys. It was fine for me as they're like brothers," Andrew remarked. "Now I have a wife, and there's a child too."

Gwen smiled, relieved she was wrong about the secret family. "Is there a free bed in this bunkhouse?"

"Yes, of course," Andrew responded.

"I was the oldest of ten, which made things tight or, as my mother described it, snuggly. We only had three bedrooms. We kept piling up, although we all had a bed, which made things manageable. Privacy is not something I'm accustomed to having. If I have the respect of the cowboys, I don't think there will be a problem," Gwen said.

"They'll treat you with respect because you're my girls. If not, they'll end up sleeping under the stars outdoors at night and shoveling manure during the day," Andrew promised.

She had never been someone's girl before, with the exception of her father, and it was something she could get used to. Gwen just smiled and turned her head to the sun. The land had a pleasant glow as it began its march toward the horizon. It was warm like it was in July back home, and she couldn't imagine Texas in a few months. But, she supposed that, like anything else, she would get used to it.

She looked at Sara in her arms, who had grabbed Gwen's finger. She had never felt so responsible for another and wondered if it was the same as her mother had felt. Gwen had figured she'd be eager to pass along Carrie's daughter, but now she couldn't imagine letting go.

"The boys know you're coming, and when they see the baby, they'll be surprised. Don't take offense if they seem suspicious at first, but I'll explain everything. Some of the cowboys have families that they've been away from for months, so I imagine they'll love having a nipper around."

"I look forward to meeting them. Does Colt see his daughter, Sally, often?" Gwen asked.

"Every chance he gets. He loves Sally, and there isn't anything he wouldn't do for that girl or for anyone he calls a friend. I'm lucky to be one of them," Andrew pointed out.

"It's important to have friends like that, and that's the kind of friend I aim to be."

"I have a confession to make," Andrew said.

"What's that?" Gwen asked.

"I'm already used to having Sara around, and falling in love with the girl is going to be easy. I had a hard time understanding the love Colt feels for Sally, but now everything is starting to make sense," Andrew gushed. "I don't know what the future holds, but thank you for bringing Sara into my life."

Gwen nodded. "It wasn't my plan, but I'm glad she's been welcomed with so much love. Most men would have put the orphan and me on the train back east."

A serious look came over Andrews's face. "Sara isn't and never will be an orphan.

She was loved and wanted from the moment I laid eyes on her. Please don't call her that."

"I know, it was just a word that I shouldn't have used," Gwen offered a correction.

Gwen was jealous of an innocent newborn, and she knew it was wrong to think that way. She was ashamed of herself for thinking Andrew was wrong for reacting to Sara the way he did. Gwen looked forward to being less judgmental after a good night of sleep.

Her body felt like it was still in motion on the locomotive, which perhaps affected her thinking.

Chapter Five

Gwen, Andrew, and Sara walked into the bunkroom, and jaws dropped when the ten cowboys saw the infant.

"Looks like you found your beautiful bride," Abner said.

"I did, and she's more than I could have imagined. She's brave, compassionate, and quick thinking. Oh, and she brought a baby along, who otherwise would have ended up in an orphanage. So, everyone, meet the future Mrs. Carver and Sara."

Andrew explained to the cowboys how Sara had come into the world and made it all the way to Fern. They hung on to every word and couldn't take their gazes off the perfect infant.

Gwen was filled with joy after Andrew used such flattering words to describe her. “It’s nice to see you all, and I imagine we’ll get to know each other well. But, of course, it can hardly be helped, considering we’ll be sleeping and eating in the same quarters.”

Andrew reached over for her hand and grasped it. It was the first time he had touched her intentionally, and she felt over the moon. Gwen felt like they were going to be a family, even though a couple of days ago, Gwen hadn’t met Andrew, and Sara hadn’t been born.

Mrs. Galloway had always said the most painful events can bear happiness if appropriately managed.

“What’s the long face for, Abner?” Andrew asked.

"I worked hard to create a great space at the end of the bunkroom for you and Miss Gwen. Unfortunately, I hadn't accounted for a baby," Abner said.

Gwen spoke up before Andrew was able. "There is plenty I need help with, and you might be able to help. Sara will wake up in minutes with her mouth open like a little bird. Having not given birth to Sara, I can't feed her as other mothers do. You can fetch me a small canning jar with a lid; you'll need to poke a hole in the lid. Next, I need a medicine dropper which may be hard to find," she started to explain. Gwen was about to speak further, but Abner interrupted her.

"I know where one of those is!" Abner blurted. "It's in the main house off the kitchen, and it's an eye dropper that Mrs.

Seager uses. They keep it near the kitchen because if there's any smoke, Mrs. Seager throws a fit and calls for her maid to drop water in her eyes. Sue Ellen works in the kitchen, and she'll get it for me cuz she's sweet on me."

"Perfect, Abner. See, you were able to help, after all. Can you fill the jar with cow's milk? Then we'll save Sara from fussing too much." Gwen was caught up in Abner's excitement, and as she looked around, everyone was smiling.

Gwen handed the baby to Andrew as she went around back to use the outhouse. The stars and a crescent moon led the way. It felt odd not to have Sara within arm's length because Gwen had been either holding her or only a few feet away since she was born.

She was startled when a woman on a light-grey horse rode up alongside her. She wore a pale-green dress with ruffles, which didn't look like something one would wear while riding. It was unlike any outfit Gwen had ever worn—let alone while she was riding.

"Are you lost?" the woman asked tersely. She couldn't see the woman's face because of the dark.

"No, I had my head up looking in the stars, so it may have seemed that way," Gwen said. "I'm on my way to the outhouse."

"This is private property, and my father, Mr. Seager, owns this ranch. Do you have business here?" she asked.

Gwen noted that the woman didn't introduce herself. "I'm here at the invitation of the foreman Andrew Carver. My name is Gwen Arnold, and I'm Andrew's mail order bride."

"Oh, well, that explains things. Be careful of wild boars at night. They've been known to run through the fields after sunset." With that, the woman dug her heels into her horse and rode away.

Gwen observed that the woman's eyes were swollen as if she had been crying. She had a profound sadness about her.

When Gwen finished her business, she walked back to the bunkhouse, and the first thing she noticed was quiet. It was a surprise that Sara wasn't wailing. Surely Abner hadn't come up with a bottle so quickly.

She pushed open the door, and the cowboys were silent as they watched Andrew bottle-feed Sara. It wasn’t common to see an infant in a bunkhouse, and watching a man feed a baby was even rarer. The sight warmed Gwen's heart, and it seemed like everyone in the bunkhouse felt the same way.

“That’s something you don’t often see. I’m Colt, by the way, and I believe you already know my daughter Sally. I’m sure Andrew filled you in while on your visit to the Duffy farm.” Colt shook his head. “There’s nothing Grace and Charlie won’t do to help someone, and it appears that goes for someone they hardly know.”

“I was happy that Grace was able to feed Sara, and she’s also the one who taught me how to make a bottle,” Gwen said. “I’d have a hungry infant on my hands if not for her.”

"Well, you're family now. Look at all the capable men who are going to take care of little Sara," Colt pointed out.

"It's like having ten big brothers. Poor Sara won't have any suitors because they'll be afraid."

Colt laughed but quickly covered his mouth so he wouldn't disturb Sara, who was almost asleep. Andrew was nodding off too.

"I'll show you to where you'll be sleeping. Abner thought a lady should have her privacy, and seeing you're not officially married yet, we have your bed separate from Andrew's," he said as Gwen followed him.

Colt pulled aside a sheet hung at the end of the row of bunks. Two beds were placed about three feet apart, each covered with a blanket and sheets. Gwen's bed had a pillow. At least, she assumed it was hers.

"I never expected a passel of cowboys to be so thoughtful and full of manners," Gwen gushed. "I haven't gotten so much as a sideways glance since I've been here."

"We did it for you, of course, but also for Andrew. You got yourself a gentleman, and we all feel we want to treat him with the respect he pays us," Colt said.

"Thank you for making me feel so welcome," Gwen said.

Gwen fell asleep before dinner since she was tired from the chaotic day. She had met the man she would spend the rest of her life with, and an infant had come into her life. She and Andrew had to talk about their next step concerning Sara, although she knew the little girl was forever theirs. That had been decided hours ago whether neither of them had said anything about it. She felt in her heart that Sara needed a mother, and she was it, and Andrew's eyes were that of a new father.

It was the middle of the night, and Gwen felt a weight on her arm. Andrew had laid Sara next to her because he needed a few hours of uninterrupted sleep. He placed the bottle next to her bed so she wouldn't have to travel far when Sara woke hungry.

"Gwen, are you awake?" Andrew asked in a whisper.

"I am. It's hard not to stare at Sara as she sleeps because she's so perfect. I just know Carrie is going to be looking down on her from heaven, and Sara will make her proud," Gwen whispered.

"She'll be proud of Sara and grateful to you. I know this wasn't what you expected, but you've handled it wonderfully. I promise you that things will get better," Andrew said.

"I don't think so," Gwen uttered.

"You don't?" Andrew sounded surprised when he asked.

"I'm not sure how much better they can get because right now, they feel close to perfect. You're nearby, and our daughter is in my arms," Gwen said as she looked down at Sara.

"Did you say *our daughter*?"

"I did. Do you like the sound of it?" Gwen asked.

“I love the sound of it,” Andrew replied.

Chapter Six

Andrew, Gwen, and Sara followed Colt and Abner out past the burned-out shell of a cabin. The one that burned down before Andrew ever occupied it. The boys were on horseback as Andrew held the reins to the wagon. Colt had told them that they had a surprise for the three of them, and they weren't about to turn that down. Andrew and Gwen had no idea what was in store for them.

"I didn't like surprises much before you surprised me with Sara. Now I'll take them whenever they're offered," Andrew said.

"Everything has been a surprise since I left Dartmouth. I didn't expect Sara, and I didn't know I'd be living in a room full of cowboys," Gwen said. "I think if I had heard either, I would have remained in Massachusetts with my family. That would have been a huge mistake because now I wouldn't change a thing."

"I wouldn't change a thing either. With you and Sara, I feel that I have the family I was afraid to dream of. We haven't spent a great deal of time alone, but I've seen you grow into a wonderful mother, and you go out of your way to be kind to the men. Most of the cowboys who work with me are looked over by beautiful women like you. I'm impressed by the way you treat every one of them. I hope you know how glad I am that you came as my mail-order bride and no one else."

Gwen felt her face warm. There were times that Gwen wasn't sure Andrew found her helpful or attractive in any way. He had a child, and she feared that was all he wanted and that she was no longer in use.

"Thank you for your kind words. I'm glad you don't regret your decision to get a mail-order-bride in the first place," Gwen said.

"I'd be crazy to have regrets when a beautiful woman has entered my life," Andrew said.

Gwen couldn't help taking a deep breath because it was the first time anyone had called her beautiful. She couldn't find the words to respond to such a compliment, but she didn't have to because Colt and Abner pulled up on their horses. They had arrived, and their surprise awaited.

The boys and Gwen stopped in from what looked a little like a shack, although a porch was added out front. All the weeds looked like they had been recently cleared, and there was even one window that looked out on the range. They tied their horses to a nearby tree, and Abner came around to help Gwen and Sara down.

"Welcome home," Grace Duffy said as she pushed open the door and walked onto the porch.

Colt stood on the front porch with Abner by his side. "We weren't sure how fast we could build you a house with all the work on the ranch. We thought this old shack would be good enough for now. We fixed some holes in the roof and put on a porch where you could sit with Sara while you're feeding her." He then looked to Grace, who had Charles on her hip. "We needed a woman's touch, so we turned to the best one we know… Grace Duffy."

"Come on up," Grace said as she reached to grab Sara so she could feed her while she was around. Gwen took Charles and couldn't believe that soon Sara would be that heavy. "I'm not so sure if I gave it a woman's touch, but it sure is clean. I had Abner clear a path to the outhouse because I could see you going at night and tripping over a tree root. It's just one room, but after the bunkhouse, it will feel like a palace."

"Indeed it will. I hope I live long enough so I can begin to repay the kindness you have shown Sara and me," Gwen said.

"I do not doubt that you would do the same. Most times, it's people who don't have a lot that give the most," Grace said. "I find that every bit of kindness I give comes back to me."

Gwen looked and saw Andrew thanking Colt and Abner, which allowed her to ask Grace questions. "I saw a woman on horseback the other night while I was behind the bunkhouse. She didn't introduce herself, and she was Mr. Seager's daughter."

"Was she wearing a dress with porcelain skin?" Grace asked.

"Yes, and she was about my age. She wasn't rude, but she didn't introduce herself, and she seemed to have been crying. Her eyes were swollen and her face blotchy. Should I be concerned about this woman?" Gwen asked.

"It was Lottie Scoggins, the only daughter of Mr. and Mrs. Seager. She has always been kind, and my little sister knew her well when they were young. Lottie used to sneak away and come to play at our family farm. Her mother was very strict, and her father rarely noticed her because he was busy running the ranch," Grace explained.

"Is her husband unkind? Why would she be crying when she seems to have everything a person could desire?" Gwen asked

"Leland Scoggins is a good man, but rumors are that she's been unable to conceive a child, and it's been three years. All she ever wanted was to be a mother, and it's the one thing all her father's money cannot buy."

"I knew there was a story behind the woman's sadness. I will think of Lottie before I complain about Sara crying in the middle of the night," Gwen said.

"Now that we're talking about the Seager family, you should be warned to stay away from Mrs. Seager. I haven't had any interactions with her, but I've heard stories."

"Thank you for the warning," Gwen said.

Colt told Andrew he would pack up their things so they could start living as a family immediately.

Gwen stood with a sleeping Sara in her arms with Andrew next to her. Except for a few times in the wagon, they hadn't been alone as a family. They watched the others get smaller and smaller as they rode away. Finally, they looked at one another, and both let out a sigh of relief.

"There is one thing wrong with Sara that we need to fix," Andrew said.

Gwen widened her eyes, not able to think of one thing wrong with the three-week-old child. "What do you think is wrong with Sara?"

"Our little girl has to have our last name, and that will only happen if we get married." Andrew grinned.

Chapter Seven

Gwen used the fire out back for most of the cooking since there was no kitchen in the one-room shed. She had a good skillet and a stew pot, so Gwen didn't notice a big difference from cooking in Dartmouth. Sara slept in a basket kept in the shade under a tree, and Gwen would sing to her when she fussed, which wasn't frequent or prolonged. It felt very different from when she cared for her siblings at home because she was responsible for everything with Sara. She was Gwen's daughter, and the feeling was euphoric, as if Sara had been born from her own body.

Food was plentiful since they lived on a ranch with a lot of access to meat. The

Duffys' farm provided most of the vegetables they ate, and Grace had filled the shelves with canned beans and jam. A bin in the corner of the house contained more ears of corn than they would ever eat, and apples were abundant. Gwen couldn't wait to make apple pie in the skillet. Of course, it was Grace who gave her instructions on how to bake without an oven. Andrew was going to take her to the mercantile in Fern to buy flour and sugar.

Andrew came home every evening with a jug full of fresh milk for Sara. Gwen had spilled some the previous night, so he was going to drop some off on his way to the western edge of the ranch. She heard footsteps and thought he had come home earlier than she thought he would.

"Hello, I saw smoke and smelled something good, so I had Gerald pull the buggy over. I'm Thelma Seager. My husband, Roger, owns this ranch, and I've never seen you before," she said.

The woman wore a brick-red dress, and her jet-black hair was pulled back neatly. A wool hat with a pearl accent perched on her head. Gwen remembered that Grace had warned her about Mrs. Seager. However, she was confused because she appeared to be a gentle woman.

"I'm Gwen Arnold, soon to be Mrs. Andrew Carver. I've been here less than one month, and soon, Andrew and I will be married," she said cheerfully. Gwen wiped her hands on her apron.

"I heard a woman was living with the cowboys, and I guess you're the one. My daughter had an encounter with you and said you were pleasant enough. I see you have a young child, and yet you say you've just arrived. How did that come to be?" Mrs. Seager asked.

Gwen began to see the side of Mrs. Seager that Grace had warned about. It wasn't anything she said but the way she looked and the tone of her voice. Her probing eyes made Gwen feel unsettled. She placed her hand on her hip, squinted her eyes, and pursed her lips as she waited for a response. Gwen instinctively felt protective of her daughter in the basket. She moved closer to her infant.

"She's our daughter – me and Andrew, I mean. She was left to me on the train as I was coming from Massachusetts," Gwen said.

"I see. Are you saying there was no formal adoption?" she asked as she cocked her head.

"No, it was nothing like that. It's a long story, but Sara needed a home, and we provided one." Gwen said.

Sara began to fuss, and Gwen picked her up out of the basket.

"This is the home you were referring to?" Mrs. Seager asked.

Her beady eyes darted from the one-room shack to the basket she was using as Sara's bed. They landed on Gwen, and she looked her up and down. Gwen knew she appeared disheveled compared to how Mrs. Seager was dressed.

"Yes. Colt, Abner, and some of the others polished up this old shack as a place for us to live. It's small but happy, and I enjoy cooking in the outdoors. It's better than a stuffy kitchen." Gwen tittered nervously.

Mrs. Seager stood close to Gwen and touched Sara under the chin.

"She seems healthy. Does she have all the necessary body parts?" she asked.

"I believe so. She has all her fingers and toes if that's what you're referring to," Gwen responded. The question seemed like an odd one.

"Interesting. I'll be calling again when Andrew is present since I have questions for him. Good day, Gwen."

She turned on her heel and sashayed back to her buggy. Gwen was left with an uneasy feeling.

***

Sara slept in the basket between Gwen and Andrew as they rode in the wagon. They were on their way back from the courthouse where they were married. It was not an elaborate ceremony like the one Lottie Scoggins had likely had, but it was perfect. They went to the courthouse as Andrew, Gwen, and Sara, and they returned as the Carver family.

Andrew reached over Sara and picked up Gwen's hand. "We're married. I wish it was a fancy wedding, but it will have to do for now. Are you happy?"

"Yes. I've never been so happy," Gwen said. "I'm still concerned about the visit from Mrs. Seager. She made me feel like I was doing something wrong."

Andrew nodded and scowled. "Don't be intimidated by that woman. If anyone is doing anything wrong, it's her. She has nothing better to do but harass those that she thinks she's better than. You gave a child a mother when she had none. You should be praised more than anything else, and now you're my wife. I won't allow anyone to harm you."

"I don't know what I did to deserve a husband like you. No one has made me feel as safe as you do. Colt told me what a good person you are, and it didn't take long for me to figure it out myself," Gwen gushed. "He said you're the best foreman in the entire state of Texas."

The Carver family stopped at a stream before heading home. Andrew thought it would be a good idea to have fish for dinner, and Gwen agreed. She imagined they were still wearing heavy coats in Dartmouth and maybe bearing down for the last snowfall of the season. Gwen felt the warm breeze and knew Texas was her forever home. She sat on a rock with Sara asleep in her arms.

Andrew came up behind her and kissed Gwen on the cheek. "I picture the day when we'll have a real house with a kitchen and a bed where Sara will have big dreams that we'll try to make come true."

"Sounds like a dream and one that I know you'll make happen. Sara is lucky to have you as a father, and I'm fortunate to have you as a husband."

The sun was reflecting off the gurgling waters onto the dainty pink flowers lining the shore. Sara was cooing, and all seemed right in the world.

"Gwen, the feelings I'm developing for you are strong and unexpected. I didn't imagine I would ever feel this way, and I need to know if you feel similar."

Gwen smiled. "I was hoping you felt the same. I wasn't sure if I could feel this way after knowing someone just one month and thought I was just having silly romantic notions."

“I don’t think love can be compared to a silly romantic notion,” Andrew said as he looked into her soul with his endless green eyes.

“Love?” Gwen asked. Her eyes filled to the brim with happy tears.

“Yes, Gwen Carver. I love you, and I will remain by your side until the end of my days.”

“I love you too, Andrew.”

Their lips met, and they kissed. Sara made a noise, and they looked down to see what they were sure was a smile. They laughed.

Chapter Eight

Sara slept in a cradle Grace had brought over earlier in the day. Andrew and Gwen finished a dinner of chicken stew that he said was the best he'd ever had. Gwen looked up when she heard familiar footsteps. They were those of Thelma Seager.

Gwen stood, but before she could warn Andrew, Mrs. Seager came around the corner.

"Hello, Andrew. I assume this woman who is to be your wife told you of my visit the other day," she said.

"She did, and if it's about us living in the shack, I assure you that it was approved by Mr. Seager. Colt, one of the cowboys, asked him personally," Andrew explained.

"Gwen is now my wife. I was lucky that she married me only days ago. Along with Sara, we are a family."

"At least you have the honesty to call this place a shack. Your wife referred to it as a home, house, or some other nonsense. You are free to live here, but it won't be with your stolen baby. We are a country of laws, and you can't just call any baby your own and raise it in filth."

Gwen turned red with anger, and Andrew did the same. Any home would be small when compared to the Seager Mansion, and Gwen was proud of the place her family called home. Mrs. Seager crossed her arms and stood with authority.

"You can't just tear a child from the only home she's ever known," Gwen said.

She didn't cry because she wouldn't give Mrs. Seager the pleasure of seeing her reduced to tears.

"My daughter has a beautiful home, and she's married to Leland Scoggins, a wealthy attorney. Their house is ready for a child such as the girl you call Sara. Any court in the land would award Lottie and Leland the baby. She has as much claim on the girl as you do, but her circumstances are much more favorable," Mrs. Seager explained. She walked toward Sara as if she were going to be allowed to just take her away.

"I'm sorry, Mrs. Seager. I will not allow you to take another step toward my daughter," Andrew said in a stern voice.

"Fine. I will come back in two days, and I will not be alone. It will allow time for

Lottie to collect last-minute items for her baby." Mrs. Seager looked down at a sleeping Sara.

"No, she's my daughter," Gwen said loudly.

Mrs. Seager pointed her finger at Gwen. "Now you listen to me; the baby will leave this shack, and if not by me, then by the authorities who will whisk her away to an orphanage. Either way, the baby will no longer be in your care."

Just as she did before, Mrs. Seager turned on her heel and disappeared into her buggy. They stood in stunned silence for less than a minute before Andrew shattered the quiet.

"When she pointed at you, it took tremendous control not to knock her down, but I remembered what my mother taught me. I never raise my hand to a woman. I learned that when I was twelve years old, and I live by it to this day."

"I'm glad you didn't strike her even though she earned it by the way she came in here. What are we going to do?" Gwen asked. Now that she was gone, the tears freely escaped her eyes. "If she takes Sara, it will be like taking my beating heart. Our daughter doesn't care if we live in one room…all she cares about is being loved."

Andrew paced the floor. "You said it, sweetheart. All we need is love. The three of us will survive together regardless of the circumstances. We are going to run, and we have friends that can help us escape. We can't take the horses or the wagon from here because they belong to the Seagers, and I'm not a thief. I won't steal their horses, and I didn't steal my daughter."

***

Andrew, Gwen, and Sara showed up at the Duffy home. Colt went along, too, because he wanted to see his daughter Sally.

Charlie answered the door. "Come in. Grace is reading a bedtime story to the children who still believe in fairy tales. Colt rode over earlier and told us about Mrs. Seager and Sara."

"Just so you know," Gwen said as she cradled Sara in her arms, "I believe in fairy tales, and I was living one until all this happened. In a month, I married a man I loved, and my beautiful daughter came into my life. Not bad for a mail-order bride. I would like my fairy tale back."

Grace walked in with a squiggly Charles in her arms. "Welcome. Charlie and I have talked this over and have come up with a plan. Leave tonight with our wagon. Go home in the dead of night and pack what you can. The men working for Mrs. Seager will come here looking for you, where they'll find their wagon."

Charlie took it over. "Grace will break out in tears…fake ones because she doesn't often cry." He chuckled. "She'll say you headed to California, but first, you were stopping in Midland to visit distant relatives. I won't tell them you took our wagon."

“Sounds like a plan. The men looking for us will head to Midland, a town where we have no intention of going. They’ll never find us, because we’re heading north. There must be work in Kansas or even Dakota territory.”

Sara began to fuss, and without saying a word, Grace took her in her arms.

“I’ve come to rely on your friendship and your generosity in feeding Sara. We will be lucky to find friends along the way that are half as good as you,” Gwen said.

“We’ll think of a way we can get repayment for the wagon to you," Andrew said.

Charlie laughed. “You don’t owe me a thing. We’ve forged a friendship that you can’t place a price on. Just be sure to do a kindness for someone else.”

Grace handed a few dollars to Gwen. "A woman needs to keep a little something for herself. If you're going north, you might run into cold weather. Buy a wool outfit for Sara because I didn't have time to knit one for you."

"Thank you. I'll buy yarn at the mercantile on our way out of town. It will give me something to do while Andrew is holding the reins. I'll miss you." She hugged Grace with her free arm.

It was going to be dark by the time Andrew, Gwen and Sara arrived home. Even if Mrs. Seager had spies, they wouldn't notice the activity after dark. Gwen would allow Sara to sleep a couple of hours, and she would box up any food they could take with them. Andrew planned to stop in the bunkhouse and say farewell to the cowboys, who had become like family.

Chapter Nine

Andrew hitched his horse to a tree behind the bunkhouse. He stopped for a moment to look at the structure that he had called home for almost ten years. It had been a considerable part of his life, and the men inside were like brothers. Every one of them had a unique role in the brotherhood, and when one left, their absence was felt. Andrew was no different, but he had faith that they'd survive just fine without him. Colt was a strong leader, and the men would listen to him.

He pushed open the door to find a few playing cards and the others gathered around as they watched. They all looked up when Andrew walked in.

"Look who decided to join us," Norbert said. He had been the cook for the men in the bunkhouse for years. He never failed to please.

"Were you dealt a losing hand again?" Andrew asked. "For the life of me, I don't know why you bother playing when you never win. You could live four lifetimes, and you'd never make enough to pay everyone back," he joked.

"I'll never stop playing. I'm having more fun playing cards and losing than if I weren't playing at all."

Andrew pulled up a stool and sat down. The cowboys gathered because they knew he had something important to say.

"Colt told us you're leaving," Abner said stoically. "I don't know how this place will manage without you."

"You'll manage, and when Colt becomes foreman, which I'm sure he'll become, you obey his word. I taught him everything I know, so things won't be a lot different," Andrew said.

"What if Mr. Seager brings in a new foreman who gets rid of us all. I've seen it happen," Barney said. "Foremen like bringing in their own men."

"Mr. Seager is a good man, and he knows he has a strong crew of cowboys. Roger ain't going to change what's working so well. Now listen, I came here to say goodbye but also to ask you a favor," Andrew stated.

"All you have to do is ask," Colt said.

"I need you all to stay quiet about knowing I was leaving. The last thing I want to happen is one of you getting in trouble for my deeds. I know you're a loyal bunch, and I've never needed you on my side more than now. Most of you don't know where I'll be heading, and I'm going to keep it that way. I don't care if you let slip that I was heading west – California, maybe. I say that only because I won't be heading there. Can I count on you boys?"

There were shouts of allegiance, and they all nodded in agreement. Colt handed Andrew an envelope.

"We took up a collection. It's mainly money for cards or whisky, which we can do without. A little money might help where you're going," he said.

Andrew wasn't going to shed a tear in a roomful of cowboys. He'd never forgive himself. "Thank you, gentlemen, and don't ever forget that's exactly what you are."

They all stood a little taller when Andrew walked away, and he thought he saw a couple of them wipe away a tear. He didn't cry but surely would as he moved along the trail home to Gwen and Sara. Home wasn't the one-room shack anymore. It was wherever his wife and child were.

Gwen was feeding Sara a bottle when Andrew walked in the door. She had loaded the jars of food that lined the cupboards and tucked in a couple of extra bottles for Sara.

She would surely miss her daily visits from Grace with the yummy milk.

"We'll leave early tomorrow, and we'll have a day before Mrs. Seager even realizes we're gone," Andrew said. "Are you ready?"

"Yes. While you were gone, I wrote a letter to my family in Massachusetts, which I'll post before we leave. I want to pick up a few things at the mercantile, and I thought we'd stop there before we head north. The wagon is covered, and no one will see that we have the entirety of our belongings packed."

"We can do that. I love Fern, Texas, and doing this to Mr. Seager is difficult, but I love you more," Andrew professed. "Colt is capable and organized, and he's never leaving Fern. I think Roger Seager knows that, and he'll take over as foreman as soon as I leave."

"Don't you have your weekly meeting with Mr. Seager tomorrow?" Gwen asked.

"Thanks for remembering, but I think I'll skip it. I'm going to have a hard time pretending things are normal," Andrew said.

"I think you should go to the meeting so you don't arouse suspicion. I'm surprised Mr. Seager hasn't told his wife that what she's doing is cruel," Gwen said.

"You've seen the size of that house; they don't see each other too often, and it's likely that he doesn't know about her scheme. It's not for me to get involved in their marital relationship," Andrew said.

"I was thinking about Mrs. Seager, and I don't think she's a horrible person. I would do anything for Sara if she needed it. I can't say I would steal a baby for her, but who knows," Gwen said.

"You amaze me, Mrs. Carver. A woman threatens to take away your child, and you still manage to find the good in her." Andrew leaned in and kissed her.

"I'm no saint since I'm still hopping mad. I was just trying to see her side of things, and her view is different from ours. Does she have any children besides Lottie?"

"The Seagers had two boys. One married a rancher's daughter and lives across the state. The other is a lawyer in Washington, DC. Mrs. Seager is likely bored with only one of her children remaining, and she can't help meddling in her business."

"See, kindness is contagious. You're also finding excuses for Mrs. Seager's behavior," Gwen teased and smiled. Sara reached up and grabbed a chunk of her honey-colored hair.

"I'll make my way up to the house for my meeting with Mr. Seager in the morning, and we can leave when I return," Andrew said.

***

Andrew walked up the grand steps of the Seager mansion and was met by Harold, the butler. He had joined the cowboys in the barn for an occasional game of cards when he wasn't at work. Harold was friendly and professional as he led Andrew down the hallway. He knocked and then opened the door to find Roger Seager with his feet up on the desk. He was gazing out the window at the pasture.

"Andrew, right on time as always. Take a load off, young man," Roger said. He didn't require he be called Mr. Seager, especially when it was just the two of them in his office.

"You look well. I don't have anything bad to report. We fixed the fence on the western edge of the ranch where you suspected outlaws were getting in. There was some evidence that they had set up a temporary camp down there, so I have a few men go out there every week. That way, we let the outlaws know we're there," Andrew explained.

"Good. I know it's a big place, but we have to make sure none of it is neglected. Outlaws are waiting for us to get lazy," Roger said. "If you need to hire more men, just let me know. Colt says you can get it done with the men you have, but I wanted to make sure."

"If Colt says it, it's true. There are times I think he's a better cowboy than I am," Andrew said. He was laying the groundwork to get Colt promoted when he left.

"Nah, I don't know what I'd do without you. If there's anything you ever need from me, just ask. You're the reason my ranch is as profitable as it is."

Andrew gave him the rest of the progress report, and Roger told stories before Andrew left. He almost said something about

Mrs. Seager, but he couldn't be sure how that would go. The plan he and Gwen had in place was a good one.

Chapter Ten

"I can't believe we're leaving," Gwen said as they pulled away from their small home. It would remain a special place in her memories because it was where they grew to be a family.

"No looking back now," Andrew said. "I'll find work wherever we go since I'm not afraid of long days, and I'm still young. Did you tell your parents the whole story about why we're leaving Texas?" he asked.

"No, because I didn't want them worried. They wouldn't be able to do anything from far away, and I'd rather them think there are no problems. My mother fretted about me becoming a mail-order bride. I told her everything would work out, and I think it did. Would you like me to read what I wrote?"

"Sure, if you care to share," Andrew responded.

"Of course. I'll read you a portion of it, so you don't get bored."

...After Andrew accepted Sara as his daughter and I did, too, we settled into our first home. It's small but splendid, and its size means that I never have to be far from the ones I love. I am truly happy in Fern, Texas, and in my wildest dreams, I never imagined my life would turn out this happy. I wake up each day with a smile on my face and thank the Lord that Andrew and Sara are in my life.

Gwen folded the letter and resealed the envelope when they pulled near the mercantile.

"Are you alright taking Sara in with you?" Andrew asked. "I'd like to close my eyes because I'm fixing to push ahead until we get out of Texas. I'll be holding the reins through the night."

"I'm fine. I'll stop in at the post office before I pick up a few things for Sara. Rest easy," Gwen said as she kissed her husband on the cheek.

Gwen walked into the mercantile with Sara sleeping in one arm. She had perfected holding her securely with one arm so she could get things done with the other. The way Sara was eating meant that soon she wouldn't be able to support her with one arm only.

The mercantile stocked goods for three surrounding townships, so they had a wide variety of goods. Grace told her it was better than those in most small towns. Gwen had only been in the store once before, but she remembered the kind woman behind the counter.

“Hello, Mrs. Templeton. I’m going to mail a letter and then pick up a few things for Sara.” Gwen placed her letter on the counter so she could show Sara off to Mrs. Templeton.

“Oh, how she’s grown in only a few weeks. Feel free to look around, and I’ll hold Sara if you like,” Mrs. Templeton offered.

“That would be delightful. I brought her bottle in if she appears hungry.” Gwen pulled the funny-looking but very useful bottle from her coat pocket. “A friend taught me how to make the bottle, which works fabulously. I think it's even better than the fancy glass ones for sale."

"We can't even get those in stock. I have to send folks to the city to buy them," she noted.

A woman with a pretty blue dress and a familiar voice that Gwen was unable to place joined them at the counter. "Did you just mention glass baby bottles?"

"Yes, but we do not have them. The ones we tried to get broke on account of the bumpy roads required to travel to Fern. I know of a store in Houston that carries them," Mrs. Templeton said.

"I need mine tomorrow because that's when my baby girl arrives," she said.

Gwen glanced at her belly. "Are you adopting a child?"

"In a way, yes. She's supposed to be about the age of your sweet girl. Is motherhood as wonderful as it sounds?" she asked.

"Better than anything you could imagine. There is nothing in the world I wouldn't do for my daughter. Every breath I take and every decision I make is done with her in mind," Gwen said.

Suddenly, she remembered where she had heard the voice before. It was behind the bunkhouse on the night she arrived in Fern. She was talking to the woman who was supposed to receive her child.

"It gives me shivers to hear you speak of the love you have for…" She paused because she didn't know the name.

"Sara. Her name is Sara, and I'm Carrie from Oklahoma," Gwen lied.

"I'm Lottie Scoggins, and you're familiar. Are you sure we haven't met before?"

"No, and goodness, look at the time. My husband has been waiting for me, and I must go," Gwen said.

Lottie had no idea the lengths her mother had gone to. She seemed like a genuinely nice person, and Gwen was sorry that she would end up hurt.

"What about the things you were going to pick up?" Mrs. Templeton asked as Gwen grabbed Sara and ran towards the wagon. She saw Andrew was sleeping, so Gwen stopped to gather herself and catch her breath.

"Gwen, stop!" Lottie called out from the mercantile steps. "You left this letter on the counter. And now I recognize you. You're the woman from the bunkhouse who I was rude to."

"I don't know what you're talking about. I have to go," Gwen said as she started to walk more quickly.

"Things are falling into place, and I think we were meant to run into each other. Sara is the baby my mother said was willingly being given to me. That wasn't true at all, was it?"

"No, and if you have any compassion, you'll let me and my family go. Please," Gwen choked as the words came out. But she had stopped and turned to answer Lottie's questions.

"I can't let you go. The return address on the letter was from Mrs. Andrew Carver; your husband is like a member of my family. You're as sweet as can be and can't have ill intentions."

Lottie raised her hand and waved at Andrew, who was waking up.

"What's going on?" Andrew jumped from the wagon.

"A horrible thing is being done to you and your wife. We are going to speak with my father and clear this matter up. Gwen showed me the power of a mother's love, and I want to honor it by setting my mother straight!" Lottie exclaimed.

"I missed something big. It looks like we're turning around, Gwen, because I wouldn't want to go against Mrs. Scoggin's wishes," Andrew said. He was still dazed from his nap

"I'll see the two of you up at the house first thing in the morning," Lottie said as she marched back to her buggy, and her driver whisked her away.

Chapter Eleven

"Dinner tonight with the Duffy family will be a celebration that I thought we'd never have," Gwen chirped. "Lottie said our meeting was meant to be. I never believed in such things, but this one makes me think."

"How so?" Andrew asked.

"I think Carrie was looking out for her little girl from heaven. At least it's a nice way to see things," Gwen said.

"I should have said something to Roger during our meeting yesterday. I hope he understands that my predicament was delicate, and I couldn't chance him telling his wife."

Andrew laced his arm around Gwen's free arm, and she carried Sara in the other.

They walked up the steps that he had already scaled many times. It would be the first time Gwen had been inside a mansion, and she wished she had a nice dress to wear.

"I've never been so nervous. What if this is all a trick, and Sara will be taken from us?" Gwen fretted.

"Don't be silly. The Seagers are good people for the most part, and they wouldn't play that kind of game." Andrew leaned over and kissed her cheek. "You look beautiful. You don't have to say a word if you don't want to."

Before she could say another word, Harold, the butler, answered the door. "Follow me into the formal dining room. Mr. and Mrs. Seager are waiting to receive you, and so are Mr. and Mrs. Scoggins. Don't worry, Mrs. Carver. You did nothing wrong."

They went in and sat next to each other on a blue velvet couch. Sara slept, and Gwen brought her bottle just in case she fussed.

Mr. Seager spoke first. "Aren't you a perfect little family. There's a warmth coming off you, and to think that was threatened by a member of my family. I meant it when I said this ranch's success is in large part due to you."

"Thank you, sir. We just want to return to living our quiet life in the small house. We know it isn't much, but it's clean, and all Sara's needs are met. We don't even need an apology because we understand a mother's love for her daughter got out of hand."

Gwen nodded in agreement.

"I'm not going to speak for Mrs. Seager, but I'm hoping she has a few words to share." He nodded toward his wife.

Thelma Seager crossed the room and sat next to Gwen. "I was wrong to think I could walk into your home and threaten your family. I wanted my daughter to have the same happiness you have, and I was wrong to take yours so I could give it to Lottie. Lucky for me, my daughter has a heart the size of Texas and showed me the error of my ways." She covered Gwen's hand with hers. "I'm sorry, Gwen. Please forgive a silly old woman who should have known better."

"I forgive you, and you're welcome to come visit my humble home anytime you want," Gwen said with a smile.

"I will, and is there a chance I can hold your adorable daughter?" Mrs. Seager asked.

"Yes, and you can use this bottle to feed her also. A friend borrowed your eye dropper to make it… I'll be sure to replace it someday," Gwen said.

Mrs. Seager laughed. "I thought I had lost my eye drops. Don't worry about it. Sara needs it more than I do."

"Leland and I are going to the orphanage in Houston first thing tomorrow. No more shenanigans. We're ready to welcome a child into our home," Lottie said. "I don't know why we didn't do it sooner. Gwen, you inspired me."

"Glad to do it. Your baby and Sara can grow up together," Gwen said with delight.

"I have one more thing. It's about your small house, which I'm sure is perfect. However, I want my foreman to live closer to the house, so we can confer. We have two guesthouses out back, and you can have your choice," Mr. Seager offered. "They're each four-bedroom houses. Do you think you'll be willing to fill them up?"

"Without a doubt," Gwen blurted. "I'm from a big family, and I want at least six children."

"Six?" Andrew asked, and the room fell silent. "I was thinking at least eight."

They all laughed, and for the first time, Sara did too.

The End

FREE GIFT

Just to say thanks for checking our works we like to gift you

Our Exclusive Never Before Released Books

100% FREE!

Please GO TO

http://cleanromancepublishing.com/gift

And get your FREE gift

Thanks for being such a wonderful client.

Please Check out My Other Works

By checking out the link below

http://cleanromancepublishing.com/fjauth

Thank You

Many thanks for taking the time to buy and read through this book.

It means lots to be supported by SPECIAL readers like YOU.

Hope you enjoyed the book; please support my writing by leaving an honest review to assist other readers.

.

With Regards,

Faith Johnson

Printed in Great Britain
by Amazon

33197646R00067